The Case of the Glow-in-the-Dark Ghost

D1400841

Read all the Jigsaw Jones Mysteries

The Case of the Glow-in-the-Dark Ghost

by James Preller
illustrated by Jamie Smith
cover illustration by R. W. Alley

A
LITTLE APPLE
PAPERBACK

SCHOLASTIC INC.
New York Toronto London Auckland Sydney
Mexico City New Delhi Hong Kong Buenos Aires

*With apologies to Shaggy, Velma, Freddie,
Daphne, Scooby, and, of course,
the Mystery Machine.*

—JP

ISBN 0-439-55998-7

Text copyright © 2004 by James Preller. Illustrations copyright © 2004 by Scholastic Inc. All rights reserved. Published by Scholastic Inc. SCHOLASTIC, LITTLE APPLE, A JIGSAW JONES MYSTERY, and associated logos are trademarks and/or registered trademarks of Scholastic Inc.

12 11 10 9 8 7 6 5 4 3 2 1   4 5 6 7 8 9/0

Printed in China   40
First printing, August 2004

CONTENTS

Chapter One

In the Tree House

My name is Jones. Jigsaw Jones. I'm a detective. I solve mysteries.

If your socks are missing, I'm the guy to track them down. I get a dollar a day for my trouble. So here's a free hint: Try looking under your bed first.

But let's face it. Missing socks aren't very exciting. Sure, they might have holes. They might even stink like old cheese. But they won't scare you.

I'd rather track down a ghost than a pair of argyle socks.

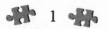 1

The thing is, I just did. Track down a ghost, that is.

Go figure.

I was sitting in my tree house just a few days ago.

My partner and best friend, Mila Yeh, was the first one up the tree house ladder. Mila was followed by a girl I'd never seen before. She wore a baggy orange sweater, a skirt, and bulky green socks.

Mila introduced us. "Jigsaw, this is Cassandra. She's the girl I told you about."

Cassandra's bangs were cut in a straight line across her forehead. And I mean a *perfectly* straight line. Her eyes were unusually large and peered out from behind extremely thick glasses. They made her look like a South American tree frog.

Cassandra's body was short and stout. Before I knew it, I was absentmindedly singing in a soft voice, *"I'm a little teapot, short and . . ."*

Mila gave me a sharp look. I stopped singing.

"Grape juice?" I offered. "Cookies?"

Cassandra said yes to both. She took a noisy gulp of grape juice and swallowed loudly. She chomped on the cookies with all the delicacy of a Great Dane.

"Mila tells me you've seen a ghost," I murmured.

I said this flatly. No feeling in my voice. I could have been talking about a stack of pancakes. But I wasn't. This girl, Cassandra Something-or-Other, claimed that she had seen a ghost.

In our school.

At night.

The story gets even better. This ghost, she claimed, *glowed* in the dark.

Spooky, huh? Maybe.

I did my best not to roll my eyes. I listened carefully and nodded when it seemed like a nod needed doing. I took notes in my detective journal. And I kept my doubts to myself.

Here's the thing: I don't believe in ghosts. But I do believe in clients. And I believe in getting paid. So I was willing to listen to Cassandra's story. What else was I going to do in a tree house in the middle of the afternoon? Ride a pogo stick? I don't think so.

Besides, Cassandra had already eaten the last of my cookies. So I shut my mouth and listened.

Chapter Two

Cassandra's Warning

"I live across the street from school," Cassandra began. "I first saw the ghost about two weeks ago."

I looked up from my journal. "You've seen this ghost more than once?"

Cassandra nodded. Yes.

"Tell me about the first time," I asked.

"It was during the witching hour."

I held up a hand. "What do you mean, 'the witching hour'?"

Cassandra leaned forward. She croaked,

 6

"You know, the hour when all the dark things, like ghosts and wizards and monsters, come out from hiding."

"What time is the witching hour, exactly?" Mila asked.

Cassandra shrugged. "It changes every night," she replied. "At least, that's what Roald Dahl says."

I was confused.

"Rolled . . . doll?"

"Yes, that's right," Cassandra noted.

Since it worked so well the first time, I repeated myself. "Rolled . . . doll?"

I'm guessing that the look on my face said something like, "Wha —?"

So Cassandra added: "He's a famous author. He wrote *Charlie and the Chocolate Factory*, *James and the Giant Peach*, *The BFG* . . ."

"Oh!" I exclaimed. "*Roald Dahl!* Why didn't you say so in the first place?"

"I thought I did."

Hmmm. Well, perhaps she did. "Don't cloud the issue with facts," I scolded, raising an eyebrow.

Mila explained. "According to people who believe in this — *stuff* — there's a time in the night when everyone is asleep."

Cassandra nodded enthusiastically. "Yes, yes. That's when the monsters come out!"

I scratched the back of my neck. "How

do you figure? You were awake at the time," I noted.

"I *was* sleeping. Then I woke up, silly," Cassandra replied. "Once the monsters are out, they can't simply disappear in an instant. It doesn't work that way."

"I see," I mumbled. But I didn't see at all. And I didn't like being called silly, either. The whole thing had me in a fog. Monsters? Ghosts? I felt like I was trapped inside a bad Scooby-Doo cartoon.

Cassandra continued. "I woke up at around ten o'clock at night. For some reason, I looked out my bedroom window. It's on the second floor. That's when I saw the ghost."

"Uh-huh," I murmured. "The ghost."

"Yes," Cassandra replied. "It was floating by the classroom windows. It moved strangely. And it was glowing."

I poured myself a tall glass of grape juice.

Cassandra explained that she's seen this ghost two other times, always on Tuesdays.

Finally, I pushed the coin jar in front of her. "We'll look into this mystery for you," I said. "We get a dollar a day."

Cassandra quickly looked at Mila.

"Er, Jigsaw," Mila interrupted, "I told Cassandra that we'd do this pro bono."

"Say what?"

"Pro bono," Mila repeated. "For free."

Cassandra smiled. "It's awfully nice of you guys."

"Yeah, awfully," I muttered.

But I guess Mila was right. A good detective can't walk away from a mystery.

Mila handed Cassandra our business card. "Call Jigsaw the next time you see anything. Anytime. Day or night."

"Even if it's the witching hour?" she asked.

"Yes, even if it's the witching hour."

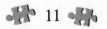 11

Chapter Three
The Cap'n and Me

I woke early the next morning and slinked into the kitchen. We had my favorite cereal in the cupboard. I wanted to eat some before my brothers beat me to it.

My sister, Hillary, was already finishing her breakfast of toast and juice. My mom sat reading the newspaper. My father stared out the kitchen window, gripping a cup of coffee as if his life depended on it.

"'Morning, Jigsaw," my mother said. My father nodded. And Hillary, who is thirteen years old, went right on talking. She went

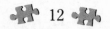 12

on and on about play rehearsals. Hillary was always in one show or another. She dreamed of becoming an actress. Hillary hoped to star in a reality television series one day. Like my older brothers Daniel, Nick, and Billy always said, if it involved Hillary getting stranded on a desert island, they were all for it.

Hillary likes to talk. Hillary is also a teenager, so her favorite subject is ... Hillary! I tried very, very hard to ignore her. After all, that's what brothers are for.

It was my lucky morning. There was still some Cap'n Crunch in the cereal box. My parents don't usually let us eat sugary cereals. They would be happiest if we ate cereal that tasted like a shoe box. But sometimes, if we beg hard enough, they will break down and buy the sweet stuff.

Get it while you can.

My dad says:

"That stuff will ROT your TEETH until

they DROP out of your MOUTH and FALL to the FLOOR like CHICLETS."

Then he says:

"Pass me the box. I think I'll have a bowl."

My mom sighs. Rolls her eyes. Frowns. Groans. Moans. Pulls her hair. (You know, the usual mom stuff.) She complains that I like Cap'n Crunch because it's "a box full of sugar-soaked cavity bombs." Okay, fine; I can't argue with that. Cavity bombs are tasty. So sue me.

But here's the thing: I like the sound they make. *Crunch, crunch, crunch!* It's like having my own private earthquake inside my mouth. I spoon in a mouthful. Then I plug my ears with my fingers. And I chew as fast and as loudly as I can.

All I can hear is the *crunch, crunch, crunch!* For a few happy moments, it's just the Cap'n and me. Sugar bombs in my mouth, exploding in my ears. Everything else falls away. No school, no worries, no ghosts. It's especially nice when my sister is talking (which, like I said, is pretty much always). I can see her lips move, but no words reach my ears. It's like hitting the mute button on the TV clicker.

Just the way I like Hillary. All picture, no sound.

Chapter Four
Another Witness

Happy with the last of the Cap'n Crunch in my belly, I headed out to the bus stop. It was a Monday morning in the middle of October. The autumn leaves were just beginning to drop from the trees. Mila was waiting at the bus stop, along with Joey Pignattano. Joey was already digging into his lunch box, busily stuffing Oreos into his mouth.

"Hi, Joey."

"Murffp, wurffle, glub," he replied.

It's hard to talk with Oreos in your cheeks. Joey looked like a chipmunk.

Mila had more to say. "I've been thinking about the ghost," she said. "We have to talk to everybody at school. We need to find out if anybody else has seen a ghost."

I scratched the back of my neck. "I don't know, Mila," I grumbled. "Maybe it was just a trick of the light. Maybe this Cassandra Something-or-Other was only dreaming."

"Jigsaw," Mila protested, "she's seen the ghost three times. And it's been Tuesday night every time. It can't be a dream."

Joey yanked on my sleeve. "Murfffph," he began, then swallowed and said, "did you say *ghost*?"

"Yes," Mila answered. "Cassandra Johnson said she saw a ghost running around our school."

"Cassandra Johnson?" Joey repeated. "I thought Jigsaw said her name was Cassandra Something-or-Other."

"Never mind that, Joey," Mila said. "Have *you* seen any ghosts lately?"

"Not lately," Joey replied. "Not ever, actually. But ghosts are invisible, aren't they?"

I shrugged. "Beats us, Joey. But you

 19

better back away from the curb. Buses aren't invisible — and here comes one now."

We climbed into the school bus and took our seats. After a few more stops, most of the gang was on board: Ralphie Jordan, Geetha Nair, Bobby Solofsky, Eddie Becker, Kim Lewis, and others. Mila asked everyone about the glow-in-the-dark ghost. Within minutes we learned that nobody

had actually seen a ghost. But everybody was sure the story was true.

Geetha Nair looked terrified. She crawled under her seat. And I don't think it was because she dropped a pencil.

"The ghost could be an old student," Eddie said.

"Yeah," Solofsky chimed in. "Somebody who died and now wanders the halls, rattling chains and flushing toilets."

Oh, brother.

Ralphie Jordan, who sat in front of me, spun around. "Earl Bartholomew told me that he saw a ghost the other day. He was riding his bike past the school at night and said he heard screams."

"Are you pulling my leg?" I asked.

"No way, Jigsaw," Ralphie answered. "I wouldn't lie to you."

"No," I replied, "but Earl Bartholomew might."

Earl was an eighth-grader who lived across the street from Ralphie. He was famous for his tall tales. Earl was not a witness I could trust.

Mila rocked back and forth. She pulled on her long black hair. That was how Mila got her thinking machine started. "I'll check out Earl's story," she said. "We have to follow every clue."

Mila was right, of course. She often was.

I turned to Ralphie. "Did Earl notice

anything . . . unusual . . . about this ghost?"
I asked.

Ralphie blinked. "You mean, besides that
it was a ghost?"

"Yeah, besides that," I said.

"Sure," Ralphie said. "Earl said that it
was dancing."

"Dancing?!" I said with disbelief. "A
dancing ghost?"

"Don't look at me," Ralphie protested.

"Talk to Earl. But there was one more thing that was a little weird."

"Yeah, what?"

Ralphie smiled. "Earl said that the ghost *glowed*."

Mila nudged me in the ribs. I hated when she did that. She had elbows like spears. Ouch.

"OK, OK," I told her. "We'll snoop around. I don't believe in ghosts. But a good detective knows that anything is possible."

Oh, brother. A glow-in-the-dark ghost. Weird witnesses. Strange shapes moving by classroom windows. It was enough to make me want a Scooby Snack.

Chapter Five

Footprints

Jingle, jangle. "Coming through! Out of the way, pip-squeaks, or I'll sweep you up with the dust bunnies!"

Mila and I jumped aside as our janitor, Mr. Copabianco, swept through the halls. A huge set of keys dangled from his belt, jingling and jangling as he walked along.

"Good morning, Mr. Copabianco!" Mila called. "How are you doing today?"

"Busy, busy! Just the way I like it!!" Mr. Copabianco answered. Then he moved on down the hall, loudly humming a bouncy tune I didn't recognize. *Da-da-da-DUM, da-da-da-DEE-da-DUM.*

That was Mr. Copabianco in a nutshell. Always smiling and happy.

We hurried to our class in room 201. Our teacher, Ms. Gleason, is really nice. She doesn't give too much homework. I like her hair best of all. It is orangey-yellow and reminds me of the autumn leaves outside our window.

Ms. Gleason is big on reading. We have to read every day in class and at home, too. I don't mind. I like books. And Mila practically *eats* books. Early in the year, Ms. Gleason decided to turn reading into a game, so she created the Amazing Author Adventure. She hung up a big game board with twenty spaces on it. You move one space every time you read a book. Once you read twenty books, you become a member of the Triple A Club. That means one very good thing: a special prize at our class pizza party!

Most spaces on the board are blank. That means you can read any book you want. Sometimes a space says, "Read a book by Mary Pope Osborne, Matt Christopher, or Beverly Cleary." Box number 17 says, "Read a book recommended by

Ms. Gleason." I can't wait to get to box number 10. It reads, "You've read ten books. That's really neat. Stop by my desk for a treat!"

Unfortunately, Ms. Gleason likes rules. It's a thing I've noticed about teachers. Go figure. The books we choose have to be chapter books at least sixty pages long. We also have to complete five bonus projects during the school year. And even though we can choose our own books, Ms. Gleason also gave us a long list of good authors. Whew. It gets pretty complicated. Which is another thing I've noticed about teachers.

Nothing is ever easy.

Today a lot of kids picked out spooky, creepy stories. I guess we all had ghosts on the brain. After afternoon recess, Ms. Gleason read to us out loud while we lounged on the reading rug. We like that best of all. We can lie back, close our eyes, and just listen.

But no snoring!

Today Ms. Gleason read a couple of short stories from *A Dark, Dark Room* by Alvin Schwartz. Everybody jumped at the end of the title story. Lucy Hiller shrieked so loud it hurt my ears.

> *In a dark, dark house*
> *There's a dark, dark room. . . .*

I won't give away the ending, but it's a scream.

There was one other important thing that happened toward the end of the day. Ms. Gleason wanted to show us something on the projector. She asked Bigs Maloney to close the curtains. Helen Zuckerman turned out the lights.

And that's when we saw them.

There were footprints all around our classroom floor.

Footprints that glowed in the dark.

"The ghost!" Geetha Nair exclaimed. "It's *real*!"

Chapter Six
A Message from Mila

Ms. Gleason snapped on the lights. I pulled out my magnifying glass. I never left home without it. Then I began crawling around on the floor. Even Ms. Gleason got down on her hands and knees for a closer look.

At first glance, I couldn't see anything unusual. The footprints seemed to have completely disappeared in the light of day. But when I looked carefully, I could see the faintest blue-white shadows.

With Ms. Gleason's permission, I took a marker and traced an outline of the foot.

"Well, it's a big foot," Ms. Gleason concluded.

"BIGFOOT?!" Bobby Solofsky exclaimed. "BIGFOOT HAS BEEN WALKING AROUND IN OUR CLASSROOM?!"

"Get real, Solofsky." Bigs Maloney scowled. "Ms. Gleason said that it's a *big* foot. Not Bigfoot, the hairy creature that lives in the woods."

"Come over here, Bigs," I said. "You've got the largest feet in the second grade. Let's see how your foot compares."

Bigs placed his foot beside the outline of the footprint. Bigs Maloney's foot was much, much smaller.

Ms. Gleason stood up and dusted off her hands and knees. "Well, it's a mystery to me," she said.

"Not to worry, Ms. Gleason," I informed

her. "Mila and I will get to the bottom of this."

Ms. Gleason smiled. "It's awfully nice to have a pair of detectives in the classroom."

A few minutes later we were jostling near the cubbies, getting our jackets and book bags and lining up for the buses.

Mila handed me a note. It was in code.

A GHOST WITH FEET? I DON'T THINK SO!

Mila and I use codes whenever possible. In the detective business, you can never be too careful. Sure, I suppose Mila could have whispered the message to me. But where's the fun in that?

I saw that it was a backward code. Mila had been practicing for weeks, so I wasn't surprised. She taught herself how to write every letter backward. And she wrote the entire message backward, too. It started from the right and went in the wrong direction.

On the way to the bus, I ducked into the bathroom. When I held the message up to the mirror, it was easy to read:

A GHOST WITH FEET? I DON'T THINK SO!

We didn't talk much on the ride home. There were too many people around. When we stepped off the bus, I asked Mila, "Want to come over?"

"I'm going to meet up with Ralphie," she answered. "He and I are going to track down Earl Bartholomew. I want to hear more about this dancing ghost."

I nodded. "Good idea, Mila. I'm going to have a snack and go find my brother Billy. I have a favor to ask him."

Mila paused. "Speaking of snacks, Jigsaw, what's the difference between a ghost and a peanut butter sandwich?"

"Beats me," I shrugged.

"A ghost doesn't stick to the roof of your mouth!"

Groan. Mila's a great detective. But she's not exactly a laugh riot.

Chapter Seven
The Plan

I got caught in a tornado as soon as I walked into my house. My brothers Daniel and Nick were wrestling on the floor, kicking and clawing and basically having a great time. Rags was barking at them. Billy was blasting music in his room. I could tell because the walls shook. Hillary was rushing from one room to another, screaming about a lost scrunchie. And my mother was tapping her foot by the front door. I don't think smoke was actually pouring out of her ears. But she didn't look happy, either.

A typical day in the Jones house.

"Hillary, you're going to be late!" my mother bellowed up the stairs. She turned to me and quickly explained, "I'm rushing off to drop Hillary at the Steamer 10 Theater. She has rehearsal. Then I have to pick up a few groceries. Get yourself a snack and start cracking on your homework. I'll be back in a jiffy."

"Yeah, sure," I said. "Hi to you, too."

My mom looked at me and sighed. "I'm sorry, Jigsaw. It's been one of those days. How was school?"

"Fine," I replied. "A ghost has been leaving footprints in room 201."

My mom wasn't listening. "That's nice," she commented. Then she hollered, "HILLARY ELIZABETH JONES! GET DOWN HERE *NOW*!"

I leaped out of the way as Hillary jumped down the stairs and flew to the door.

"Hi! Bye!" she said.

Bam. The door slammed shut. And they were gone.

Time for a glass of grape juice. Daniel followed me into the kitchen. When Mom's not around, we all hunt for junk food. Daniel was humming as he slammed through the cabinets: *Da-da-da-DUM, da-da-da-DEE-da-DUM.*

"What's that song?" I asked. "It sounds familiar."

"I don't know what it's called," Daniel said. "But Hillary's been singing it all week. I can't get it out of my head. *'They did the bash. It was a spooky smash.'"*

Daniel stopped singing. "Hey, who finished the Cap'n Crunch?!"

"Beats me," I murmured.

I got out of there in a hurry.

I made a phone call to Cassandra. She agreed to call me the minute she saw any sign of the ghost.

"So now you believe me, huh?" she asked.

"Let's just say I'm curious. Tomorrow is Tuesday," I noted. "You saw the ghost on the past three Tuesdays, isn't that right?"

Cassandra said I was right. Tomorrow night was our best bet for catching sight of the glow-in-the-dark ghost. That is, if you can count on a ghost to keep to a schedule.

I knocked on Billy's bedroom door. After a few moments, he turned down the music and let me in.

"Hey, Worm. What's happening?" he asked.

I told him. Then I added, "I need a big favor."

"I'll help you out," Billy agreed. "No biggie."

Billy promised to be ready to drive me to school Tuesday night. "What about Mom and Dad?" he asked. "Do you think they'll let you go?"

"No," I said. "But I'll think of something."

Billy laughed. "I bet you will." Then he reached for the knob on his stereo. And the music made my ears ring.

The plan was set.

Ding-dong, arf, arf, ARF!

Mila was at the door. For reasons I'll never understand, my crazy dog thought it was the most exciting thing that had ever happened in his life.

Chapter Eight
The Great Escape

Tuesday night. The sun had set. The birds had stopped singing. Darkness had fallen. The minutes ticked past. 8:05 . . . 8:15 . . . 8:30. It felt like I had been waiting forever.

I read the notes in my detective journal. Mila had caught up with Earl Bartholomew. He told Mila he had seen the ghost. He admitted that he made up the part about hearing screams just to make the story better. Mila believed him. Like she said to me, "Let's put it this way. I believe that Earl *thinks* he saw a ghost."

I didn't know what to think. Something weird was going on in our school. Maybe somebody was pretending to be a ghost. But why? In the Scooby-Doo cartoons, it was never a real ghost or a real zombie. At the end, it was always, like, the crabby old woman dressed up as a zombie. It was never a real anything. In fact, it was usually a butler named Cavendish.

8:35 . . . 8:40 . . .

Meanwhile, I was hiding out from my parents. They were watching TV in the den, and I'm pretty sure they thought I was sleeping.

Come on, phone, I thought to myself. Please ring.

Bbbbrrring! Bbbbrrring!

Wow. Not bad.

"Hello?"

"Jigsaw, it's me, Cassandra. I can see the ghost. Hurry!"

So I hurried.

Billy was set to go. Our plan was simple. We weren't going to lie. We were just hoping to not actually tell the truth.

Soundlessly, we crept to the front door. I quickly put on my shoes and jacket. Billy and I locked eyes. "Ready?" he whispered.

I nodded. Ready.

"I'm going out!" Billy hollered from the front door. "Back in a few minutes."

"OK, fine," my mother answered from the den. Good. They were too busy with their TV show to pay attention.

Billy reached for the doorknob. Opened the door. Freedom was just a few steps away. Billy added in a soft voice, "I'm taking Jigsaw with me."

A pause.

"WHAT?"

Uh-oh.

In a louder voice: "I'm taking Jigsaw with me. Back in a flash."

"Oh, no, you're not," my dad answered.

I could hear the television click off. My parents walked into the living room.

"It's almost nine o'clock on a school night," my mother said. "Jigsaw should already be in bed."

"What's going on, you two?" my father asked.

Plan A wasn't working out so swell.

It was time for plan B.

That is: Get on my knees and beg.

I told my parents everything. And begged. I promised to be back in fifteen minutes. And begged some more. I promised to do dishes every night for a week. I promised to vacuum, too. I said please about five million times. I lost count somewhere along the way.

It wasn't pretty.

I'm not proud of it.

But it worked.

"Fifteen minutes, Jigsaw," my father said.

"Or else," my mother added.

I can't say I loved the sound of that. But, quick, it was time to go. I had to catch a ghost!

Chapter Nine
To Spy a Ghost

"Turn here on Partridge Street. This is where Cassandra lives," I told Billy.

He eased the car in front of the two-story house and parked.

From our seats, Billy and I had a clear view of the school. There was the playground, and beyond that a long row of classroom windows. All of them were dark.

"I don't see anything, Jigsaw," Billy said.

We waited another minute.

Billy reached to turn up the car radio.

 51

"Wait," I said. "Now do you see it?"

Billy leaned forward, staring intently. "I see it," he confirmed.

A blue-white shape floated across the windows in one of the classrooms. In a moment, another shape joined it. This one was different somehow — fainter, yellowish.

"Ghosts," I heard myself say.

"I'm not sure what they are," Billy said quietly. "But they look like . . . dancing lights."

And they did. Up and down, over and across. In rhythm.

Billy snapped his fingers. One-two-three, snap. One-two-three, snap. "The shapes are definitely dancing. And it's to a rock 'n' roll beat."

"What?"

Billy reached over and pushed open the passenger side door. "Go check it out. You're the detective."

"What do you mean?"

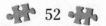 52

Billy smirked. "Go solve the mystery," he urged. "Sneak up to the window and take a closer look."

"Aren't you coming with me?" I chirped. (Yes, sad to say, my voiced *chirped*.)

"Nuh-uh," Billy replied. He turned up the radio, loud. "And hurry up," he urged. "I've got to get you home soon, or Mom and Dad will turn *you* into a ghost."

I tried to swallow, but my throat had gone dry, like I'd eaten a handful of sand.

The field was dark. The trees were shadows reaching up into the night sky. The playground was filled with dark shapes. A breeze kicked up. *Creak, squeak. Creak, squeak.* I knew that sound. The rusty tire swing.

I told myself that I wasn't afraid of any ghost.

I almost believed it.

Somehow my feet kept bringing me

closer . . . closer. I was fifty feet away, thirty feet away, ten feet away from the windows.

At first, it was just noise.

Then, music. Definitely music.

Da-da-da-DUM, da-da-da-DEE-da-DUM.

I had to smile when I heard the words: *"They did the bash. It was a spooky smash."*

Chapter Ten

The Suspect

I crept closer to the window. Suddenly, the lights went out. The room went black. I paused, bent low beneath the window.

Thinking quickly, I dashed around the corner and stopped behind a tree where I could see the front doors of the school. The parking lot was empty, except for a lone car.

Honk, honk.

It was Billy. He wanted me to come back. I waved to him, but I knew he couldn't see me in the darkness. I couldn't wait much

longer. Just as I was about to leave, I heard jingling and jangling. The big front doors opened and closed. The dark figure of a man locked the doors behind him.

He turned and walked to the parking lot. A big set of keys jingled as he walked. I heard him humming, *Da-da-da-DUM, da-da-da-DEE-da-DUM*.

Mr. Copabianco!

I stiffened behind the tree, making myself small, silent, unseen.

Could *he* be the glow-in-the-dark ghost?

Good old Mr. Copabianco?

How? And why?

A moment later I raced across the field, flying over the cool night grass. I slid into the car, and Billy hit the gas.

Ten minutes later I was in bed.

My head was a spiderweb. A tangle of thoughts.

I didn't fall asleep for a long, long time.

Chapter Eleven

Finishing the Puzzle

I awoke early.

Solving a mystery is like putting together a jigsaw puzzle. Even after the picture becomes clear, there are always a few pieces that still have to fall into place.

I needed to clear up some facts.

I found Hillary in the bathroom. She was messing around with her hair.

"Hi, Hill," I said.

She grunted in reply.

"You've been pretty busy with that play, or whatever it is that you've been doing, huh?"

 59

Hillary grunted again. "Yeah, and I've got a killer French test coming up, too."

"Tell me about your play," I asked. "What kind of character are you?"

Hillary stopped brushing her hair and looked at me. "Since when do you care?"

I deserved that. I'd been ignoring Hillary for weeks. Whenever she talked, I tried hard not to listen. And that's no way for a detective to act. I had forgotten the detective's golden rule: Zip your lips and listen.

"I do care," I said. "It's just that . . . well . . . sorry."

Hillary smiled. A bright, beautiful, toothy smile. Maybe she *would* become an actress someday. "It's community theater," she said. "I'm a witch."

"A witch?"

"Yeah. Warts on my nose, black hat, long fingernails, the works." She clawed the air like a cat. "You should come. The show is

going to be at the Steamer 10 Theater all next week."

"What's it called?" I asked.

The Frightmare on Pine Street," Hillary replied. "It's just a bunch of spooky skits, some singing, a little dancing. Maybe even a scare or two."

"Do you, by any chance, sing a song about a spooky smash?"

Hillary shook her head. "Boy, you are out of it, little brother. I've been singing that song all week."

"Thanks, Hill," I said. And for no reason at all, I gave her a quick hug.

I told Mila all about it at the bus stop. She pulled on her hair and asked a million questions.

"We've still got some detective work to do at school," I said. "But I've got a pretty good idea what we'll find."

When the bus dropped us off, we didn't go right inside the heavy doors. Instead, we walked to the parking lot. "I think this is it," I said.

"Are you sure this is where you saw his car?" Mila asked.

"Sort of sure," I said with a shrug. I handed Mila my magnifying glass. "Let's look around."

After a couple of minutes, Mila exclaimed, "Jigsaw! Look here! And here . . . and here!"

Faint blue-white shadows. Footprints. I knew that if I could turn off the sun, they'd glow in the dark.

Chapter Twelve

Dancing in the Dark

We knocked on the door to the janitor's room. We could hear Mr. Copabianco humming behind it: *Da-da-da-DUM, da-da-da-DEE-da-DUM.*

It was one of those songs you just couldn't get out of your head.

We found Mr. Copabianco sitting at his desk.

On top of the desk was a box. It was overflowing with fake plastic hands, spooky masks, fright wigs, and what looked like a dozen different Halloween costumes.

 64

"What's all this stuff?" Mila asked.

Mr. Copabianco's eyes twinkled with delight. "I'm in charge of costumes and special effects for the Halloween show at the Steamer 10 Theater!" he announced. Mr. Copabianco gestured across the crowded room. "Look at my wonderful coffin. I built it myself just last night!"

It was true. A wooden coffin leaned against a corner of the room. Happily, there was no vampire inside it.

Mila and I told Mr. Copabianco about Cassandra and what she had seen — the dancing ghosts and glow-in-the-dark footprints.

Mr. Copabianco's smile grew bigger and bigger. "Yes, yes! That's me!" he exclaimed. "I've been getting ready for the show. It's a big job," he said, nodding gravely, "being in charge of the lighting and special effects."

It was our turn to smile. He seemed so happy, so proud. So *thrilled.*

"So you've been practicing here at night?" Mila asked.

"Yes, yes, right here," Mr. Copabianco answered. "Every Tuesday, just me. It's the best place, nice and empty. I even use your classroom sometimes. Ms. Gleason, she's so nice. She lets me, no problem."

"Ms. Gleason knows about this?" I asked.

"Knows? Yes, yes — she's in the show, too!"

Now I'd heard everything. Ms. Gleason

saw the glow-in-the-dark footprints and never said a word.

Mila must have been reading my mind, because she said, "Ms. Gleason probably wanted us to have fun with a new mystery."

I guess Mila was right. Again.

"But how did you do it?" Mila wondered. "The glowing, I mean?"

Mr. Copabianco tapped the side of his head with a finger. "It takes brains, Mila. Big Copabianco brains!" Again, he laughed out loud.

He showed us the special powders and paints he had mixed. The lights, projectors, and other special effects. "It was very tricky at first. Very difficult. I wanted to use lights to make ghosts. But with this special powder I mixed — look!" He poured some on himself. "In the dark, it *glows*!"

"This must be some play," I commented.

"Yes, yes! I'm even in it, too," he said with a huge smile. "Just a very little part at the end. I'm not a big star, Jigsaw, not like your sister. No, no. It's my first time onstage. Ever! I'm very excited." He paused and patted his chest, over his heart. "But nervous, too."

"Let me guess," I said. "You play a dancing ghost."

"Ha!" Mr. Copabianco laughed. "How did you know? Yes, yes! I dance . . ."

". . . and you glow," Mila added.

"Yes, yes," Mr. Copabianco said, clasping his hands together. "You should come see me — dancing and glowing, glowing and dancing! It's wonderful!"

An idea danced in his eyes.

"Let me show you," Mr. Copabianco said.

He set up a light projector and aimed it at a wall. He rubbed more glow powder on his legs and sleeves. He put on a ghostly mask.

Then he turned off the lights.

The room grew dark. And our janitor, Mr. Copabianco, started dancing. Mila and I joined in, too. We danced around like crazy ghouls. Halloween was coming. All the pieces fit into place. Another mystery was solved.

About the Author

James Preller often draws upon his own life as a basis for his Jigsaw Jones books. Like Jigsaw, James Preller has a slobbering, sock-eating dog. Like Jigsaw, James was the youngest in a large family. His older brothers called him Worm and worse — yeesh! And so do Jigsaw's!

James and Jigsaw both love jigsaw puzzles, baseball, grape juice, and mysteries! But even though Jigsaw and James have so much in common, they are not the same person.

Unlike Jigsaw, James Preller is the author of more than 80 books for children, including *The Big Book of Picture-Book Authors & Illustrators; Wake Me in Spring; Hiccups for Elephant;* and *Cardinal & Sunflower.* He lives outside of Albany, New York, in a town called Delmar, with his wife, Lisa, three kids — Nicholas, Gavin, and Maggie — his cat, Blue, and his dog, Seamus.

Jigsaw and his partner, Mila know that mysteries are like jigsaw puzzles—you've got to look at all the pieces to solve the case!

____0-590-69125-2	#1: The Case of Hermie the Missing Hamster	$3.99 US
____0-590-69126-0	#2: The Case of the Christmas Snowman	$3.99 US
____0-590-69127-9	#3: The Case of the Secret Valentine	$3.99 US
____0-590-69129-5	#4: The Case of the Spooky Sleepover	$3.99 US
____0-439-08083-5	#5: The Case of the Stolen Baseball Cards	$3.99 US
____0-439-08094-0	#6: The Case of the Mummy Mystery	$3.99 US
____0-439-11426-8	#7: The Case of the Runaway Dog	$3.99 US
____0-439-11427-6	#8: The Case of the Great Sled Race	$3.99 US
____0-439-11428-4	#9: The Case of the Stinky Science Project	$3.99 US
____0-439-11429-2	#10: The Case of the Ghostwriter	$3.99 US
____0-439-18473-8	#11: The Case of the Marshmallow Monster	$3.99 US
____0-439-18474-6	#12: The Case of the Class Clown	$3.99 US
____0-439-18476-2	#13: The Case of the Detective in Disguise	$3.99 US
____0-439-18477-0	#14: The Case of the Bicycle Bandit	$3.99 US
____0-439-30637-X	#15: The Case of the Haunted Scarecrow	$3.99 US
____0-439-30638-8	#16: The Case of the Sneaker Sneak	$3.99 US
____0-439-30639-6	#17: The Case of the Disappearing Dinosaur	$3.99 US
____0-439-30640-X	#18: The Case of the Bear Scare	$3.99 US
____0-439-42628-6	#19: The Case of the Golden Key	$3.99 US
____0-439-42630-8	#20: The Case of the Race Against Time	$3.99 US
____0-439-42631-6	#21: The Case of the Rainy Day Mystery	$3.99 US
____0-439-55995-2	#22: The Case of the Best Pet Ever	$3.99 US
____0-439-55996-0	#23: The Case of the Perfect Prank	$3.99 US
____0-439-55998-7	#24: The Case of the Glow-in-the-Dark Ghost	$3.99 US

Super Specials

____0-439-30931-X	#1: The Case of the Buried Treasure	$3.99 US
____0-439-42629-4	#2: The Case of the Million-Dollar Mystery	$3.99 US
____0-439-55997-9	#3: The Case of the Missing Falcon	$3.99 US